MW01626103

A Crown of My Own

Securia Moore

Illustrated by Suzanne Horwitz

Printed in the United States of America
First Edition, 2019

ISBN 978-0-578-52573-0

To My Daughter

Bedtime is so fun. Before bed mommy reads me any story I choose. My favorite books have pictures of Queens and Kings with so many different beautiful shades of black and brown skin.

Mommy and daddy have always taught me that I am a Queen too. But, I was missing one thing. I didn't have a crown.

I asked my parents, "For just this one night, can I create a crown of my own like the great Queens and Kings we read about?" They looked at me, and then each other. "Pleeeease," I cried.

"Under one condition," daddy said. "Your crown should have a meaning. What will your crown represent?" Daddy said my crown should mean something to me.
25°
07:40
THU 1/1
That way it will remind me of how awesome I am!

I ran to gather the supplies I would need. I found construction paper, jewels, glue, scissors, markers, beads, stickers, you know, the fun stuff...oh and I can't forget glitter!

THE FOUNDATION
It was time to get to work.
My dad is an Architect,
so it was a no brainer for
him to cut out my crown
design for me.
GLUE
This was
what he called
the FOUNDATION!

I was so ready to dress up my crown that mommy had to remind me about the meanings. "Nyla," mommy said, "what will that bead symbolize?" as I reached for the most COLORFUL bead I could find!
I
HBCU
GLUE

HMMMM...My hair, I thought.
I loved the cute styles my mom
would do to my natural hair
like, braids, twist outs, fros
and puff balls! I love puff balls!
"So," she said, "the beads will represent
your beautiful coils!"
HBCU

While gathering beads, I ran across a SHINY jewel. "Oh, this will be perfect on my crown."

"Why jewels?", mommy asked as I searched for more to add.

I thought about it, but this time I needed help. Mommy is one of the smartest people I know so she is the perfect person to help. "It glistens, just like your skin." I smiled. My skin does sparkle with the sun when I play.

I was loving my crown so far and I was finally getting the hang of it. Then, the SPARKELING glitter caught my eye! "This is for my BLACK GIRL MAGIC!!"
BLACK GiRL MAGiC!!
GLITTER

TALENTED
CREATIVE
FEARLESS
School President
GIFTED
Spelling Bee
I can do anything I put my mind to. I am TALENTED, CREATIVE, FEARLESS, GIFTED, I am AWESOME!

For my finishing touch, I quickly drew my favorite flower. This is to remind me to always carry myself as the Queen I am! Mommy says its ok to remind yourself WHO YOU ARE.

Finally, I was all done and I had myself a crown.
My Very Own Crown!!
I held it up and couldn't stop smiling at my creation that resembled parts of me!

"So, Nyla, are you going to tell us what your crown represents," asked daddy.

With no hesitation, I said, "When I may need a reminder, it reminds me of how extraordinary I am, inside and OUT! It represents how much I love the Queen in me."

"Job well done. We love everything about you too Queen.
May I escort you to bed your highness?"

I hopped into bed with one thing in my head.

I am a Queen.

About the Author

Securia Moore was born and raised in Atlanta, Georgia. Growing up in a disenfranchised neighborhood and attending inner city schools made her realize the need for strong, positive and impactful role models for young African American youth. Today, Securia is that role model through her inspiring work as a primary school teacher who instills confidence, self-love, and a love for learning in all her students. Securia's work strives to spread the all-important messages of educating one's self, our youth and the world about the rich African history that is so often forgotten, overlooked and misrepresented.

Let's Stay Connected!

Check us out on Instagram @reigning_knowledge

Post a picture reading to your little Queen or King and tag us!

You may also email us at reigningknowledge@gmail.com

11822245R00017

Made in the USA
Monee, IL
17 September 2019